The Ant and the Grasshopper

Retold by Lesley Sims

Illustrated by Merel Eyckerman

It was a glorious summer's day.
Grasshopper chirruped and
sang sunny songs.

Ant was too busy to sing.
He huffed...
...and he puffed...
...and he g-r-o-a-n-e-d...

as he hauled food away
to his winter store.

Grasshopper smiled and
lay back on a leaf, drowsy
and dozing in the Sun.

After a while, he called out to Ant,
"You're working too hard!"

"I have to,"
Ant panted.
"There's so much to do."

"I must collect
all this food
for the winter."

"But winter is ages away,"
said Grasshopper.

"Enjoy the sunshine
with me while you can!"

"Winter may seem ages away," Ant replied,
"but it will come all too swiftly."

"If you don't work now...

...why, when the Sun has long gone and the Earth is sleeping, you will be cold and hungry."

Grasshopper laughed and sang on.

Ant huffed...
and he puffed...
and carried more corn.

Sure enough, winter crept over the Earth.
Trees stood bare against the bleak sky.
Snow dusted the fields.

Tucked up snug in his
little home, Ant looked at
his food store and smiled.

He had boxes galore, plenty to keep him fed
until the spring buds blossomed.

Outside, in a blustery gale,
Grasshopper scrunched himself up,
trying to shelter behind a leaf.

But the wind blew through his
trembling body, however tightly he curled.
His tummy ached with hunger.

At last, he fought through the wind
to Ant's house. "Ant! Help!"
Grasshopper shouted.

Ant poked his head
outside his door.

"Grasshopper! You look frozen," he cried.
"Come inside and get warm."

"Thaw out by the stove," said Ant, "and I'll make supper."

Grasshopper beamed.
    He could almost taste
        the toasted corn already.

"Thank you kind, clever Ant,"
he said, basking in the heat of the flames.
    "I promise, next summer, I'll work too!"

Designed by Caroline Spatz
Edited by Jenny Tyler

This edition first published in 2012 by Usborne Publishing Ltd.,
Usborne House, 83-85 Saffron Hill, London EC1N 8RT, England. www.usborne.com
Copyright © 2012, 2009 Usborne Publishing Ltd.